THE BONE MAN

A Native American Modoc Tale

LAURA SIMMS

ILLUSTRATED BY MICHAEL McCURDY

HYPERION BOOKS FOR CHILDREN
New York

Printed in Singapore

First Edition
1 3 5 7 9 10 8 6 4 2

The artwork for each picture is prepared using scratchboard prints.
This book is set in 16-point Tiepolo Bold.
Book design by Stephanie Bart-Horvath.

Library of Congress Cataloging-in-Publication Data
Simms, Laura
The bone man : a native American Modoc tale / retold by Laura
Simms ; illustrated by Michael McCurdy — 1st ed.
p.   cm.
ISBN 0-7868-0089-5 (trade)—ISBN 0-7868-2074-8 (lib. bdg.)
1. Modoc Indians—Folklore. 2. Tales—California. 3. Tales—
Oregon. I. McCurdy, Michael. II. Title.
E99.M7S44   1997
979.4'004974—dc20   96-7904

CORR
E
99
.M7
S44
1997

For Meliors and Louise

—L. S.

To my three great-nephews Erik, Jon, and Wil Matson

—M. McC.

In the earliest times when the world was new, a Modoc boy named Nulwee lived with his grandmother. Every summer when the berry bushes were ripe for picking, the old woman told Nulwee a tale that made him tremble.

"On the day that you were born," she would say while placing a berry basket in the boy's hands, "Kokolimalayas, the Bone Man, drank the river dry and devoured all the people except you and me. When you are old enough to be a warrior, you will bring the waters back and people will live here once again."

Nulwee was frightened of the story. He did not know how he could some-day kill the monster and bring the waters back.

"Grandmother," he asked every year, "what does the Bone Man look like?"

Her raspy voice shook as she spoke, "He is dry, gray, too ugly, and he wears a necklace made of human bones. He is as tall as a mountain and his footsteps shake the earth."

Then she would tap the berry basket and push Nulwee toward the bushes, and he knew he should not ask more questions. But one year, when he saw that he was almost as tall as his grandmother, he added boldly, "Is that the end of the story?"

"The story is not ended because Kokolimalayas the Bone Man is not dead. He is only sleeping."

"Grandmother, where does the Bone Man sleep?"

"I do not know where the monster sleeps. I only know you must be careful. When you walk, sing the old songs as I taught you. They will strengthen your heart and the earth."

Nulwee walked outside. He wanted to forget his grandmother's words. Instead of singing the old songs, he sang his childish name song louder and louder as he walked toward the bushes: "Nulwee, Nulwee, Nulwee."

Picking berries in the warm sunlight, he soon forgot her warning. He walked, singing his name, and picking berries until the basket was full.

Nulwee walked all the way to the muddy path that had once been a river. A cold wind sent a shiver down his spine. In the distance he heard a rattling sound. The earth shook. Then he remembered his grandmother's warning.

Nulwee held tight the basket of berries and ran all the way back to the house. He didn't tell his grandmother what he had heard. But, in his heart, he knew that he had awakened the Bone Man.

The very next day he returned to the riverbed. He heard the rattling sound again. The noise began like the clattering of animal hooves in the distance. It grew loud as clicking sticks. It came close like the rattling of deer-toe rattles and turtle-shell shakers. Then the cold wind blew and the earth shook.

Nulwee wanted to run away, but his feet would not listen. His teeth chattered. His knees wobbled as he saw a monster rise up on the other side of the riverbed.

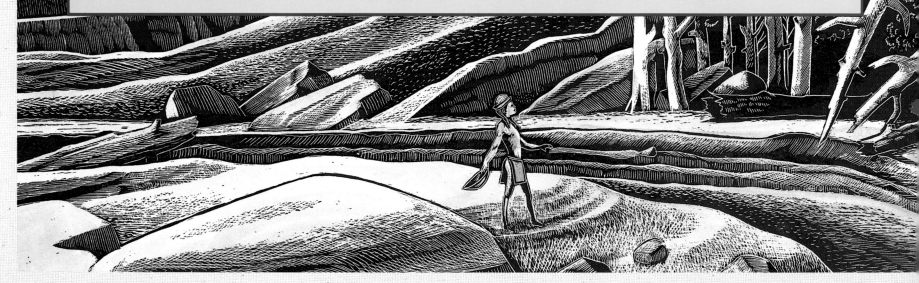

It grew, bone upon bone. He saw legs and back. He watched the long neck and round skull of the head rise up. He saw the mouth with no lips and bone teeth. It was Kokolimalayas.

The Bone Man reached out his bony hand and grabbed the berries from Nulwee's basket. He spoke, making a sound like wind racing through a hollow branch. "I'M HUNGRY!" Then he swayed and sang:

I am awake and I am hungry.
I am the Bone Man.
Sing your song.
Feed me and make me strong.

When almost all the berries were gobbled, the monster left. Nulwee ran away, back to his grandmother's house.

"What is wrong?" she asked. "Why is your basket nearly empty?"

Ashamed to have awakened the Bone Man, Nulwee answered, "The earth is too dry, Grandmother. There are very few berries."

The next day he gathered more berries, hoping that if he fed the Bone Man, the monster would not harm him and his grandmother.

As the monster ate, his bone necklace swayed. The birds stopped singing. Kokolimalayas ordered, "Nulwee, sing your grandmother's song." The boy sang. As he did, the monster grew bigger.

"Sing louder!" roared the Bone Man.

Trembling, Nulwee sang louder.

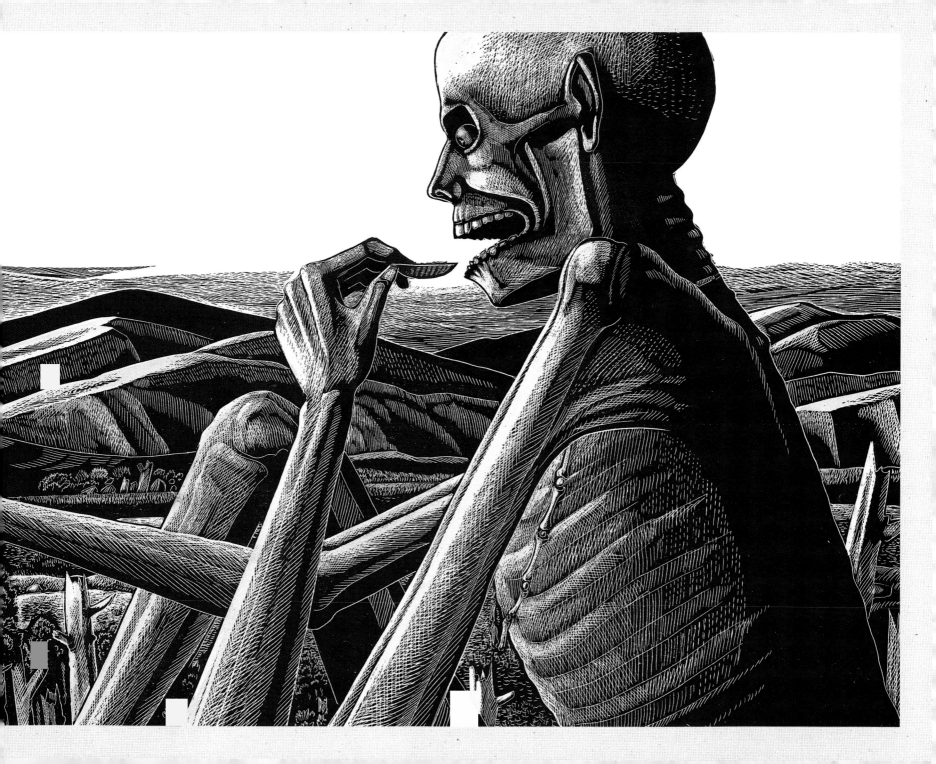

One night soon after, Nulwee's grandmother gave him a bundle wrapped in deerskin. Inside he found a painted bow and six arrows.

"These were made for you by your father. You are now old enough to become a warrior and learn to shoot."

During the day, the boy fed the monster. At night he practiced shooting the bow and arrow.

The monster was gaining strength, and as his strength grew, so did his hunger.

One day the monster emptied the basket in one gulp and roared, "I am hungry. Soon I will eat you!"

Nulwee saw the berries drip bloodlike down the Bone Man's chinbone.

The boy stood fixed to the earth with fear. He could not speak.

Kokolimalayas stretched out his arms and said, "If you were a warrior you would shoot me in the heart and kill me first. But you are just a weak child."

Laughing, the monster turned and left. The earth shook and trees in the distance bent from the force of the wind.

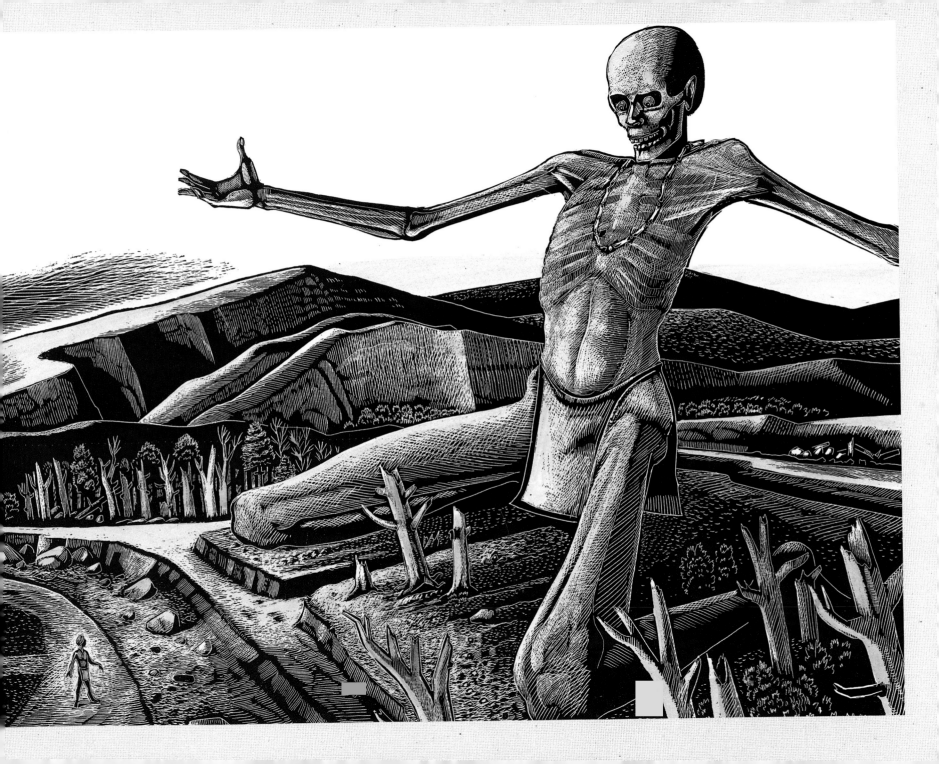

That night the old woman spoke as she pounded roots. "Nulwee, today I felt the earth shake."

He moved closer to her. Her skin smelled of sweet grass and fire. Nulwee said softly, "Grandmother, I woke the Bone Man. He says that if I do not kill him, he will kill me."

The old woman closed her eyes and swayed back and forth, thinking deeply. "You must kill the Bone Man. I have told you that since you were a baby. That is what the medicine man said when I took you to the mountains for safety the day that you were born. The day the Bone Man woke."

Under her breath, she began to sing a holy song. Nulwee was quiet.

He drank in the safety of her skin. He thought, "I must destroy the Bone Man. I cannot let my grandmother be harmed."

Finally Nulwee fell asleep. He dreamed, and in his dream the Bone Man was chasing him. Nulwee cried out, terrified, "Eat me. Do not harm my grandmother!"

His cries woke his grandmother. "You are very kind, Grandson," she said, placing her arm on his shoulder.

"I have dreamed also. In my dream I spoke to the ancestors. They told me to tell you that Kokolimalayas is strong and dangerous. But he is not smart."

Nulwee listened.

"Brave Nulwee, to kill the Bone Man you must shoot him in the heart. He will try to trick you by showing you his chest. But his heart is not in his chest. It is in his little finger."

The old woman dressed Nulwee for battle. She painted red stripes across his face, his chest, and his thighs. She carefully braided his hair and blessed the bow and arrows.

"Grandmother, I am afraid," said Nulwee.

She smiled. "A good warrior knows he is afraid and goes forward."

Nulwee stood as tall as he could. With shaking hands, he lifted the bow and placed an arrow in the notch. Then he remembered the words of his grandmother: "Your father was a good warrior. Your mother was a great medicine woman. You can call forth their strength to help you."

In that moment the boy became a warrior. He aimed his arrow at the monster's chest. Then, certain that the Bone Man was still looking up, he aimed at the monster's little finger.

Nulwee let fly the arrow. It soared like a bird. It hit like a sharp stone.

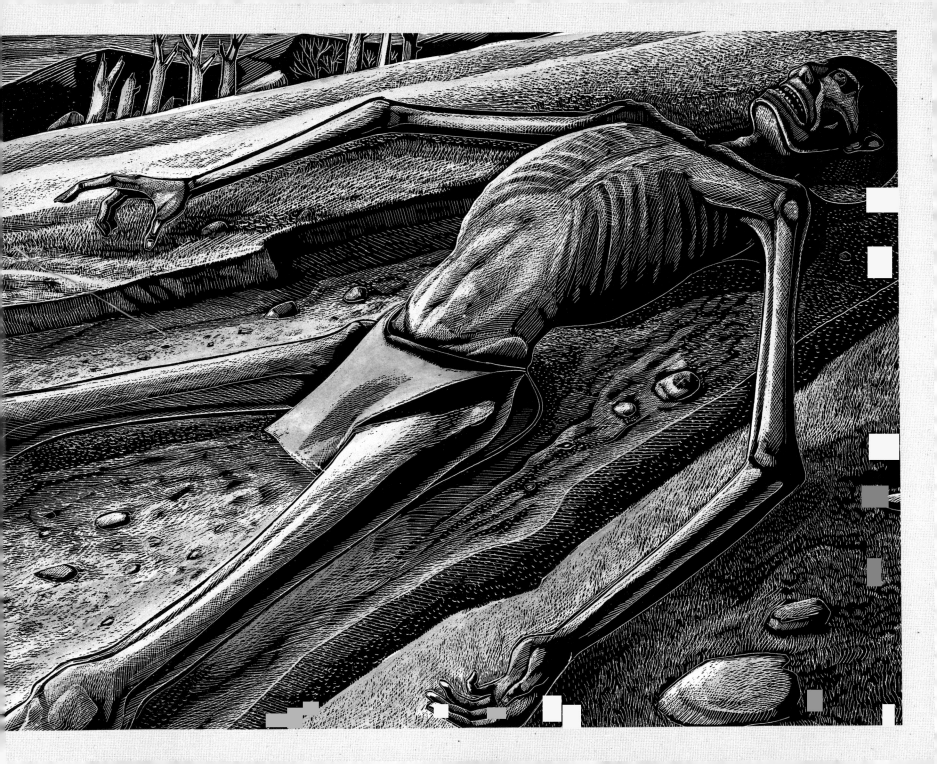

Nulwee set off for the riverbed. On the way, he sang this hunting prayer:

> *My good bow and arrows.*
> *You give me luck and strength.*
> *I am going out to hunt.*
> *I will use you well.*
> *Help me to have good luck.*
> *That's what I want you to do.*

First he filled the basket with berries. When he reached the riverbed, he sang his grandmother's songs.

The monster rose up. He swallowed all the berries. "Have you come to kill me, little warrior?" he asked, seeing Nulwee dressed for battle.

Pretending to be brave, the boy answered, "Yes. I have come to shoot you in the heart."

Smiling, Kokolimalayas lay down on the ground, arms open, and stared up at the sky. "I will make it easy for you."

Nulwee knew that the monster could break his bones like twigs. He felt sick and wanted to run away.

The Bone Man shouted, "Hurry! If you do not kill me, I will eat you!"

he Bone Man screamed, "How did you find my heart?"

Nulwee saw the heart fly from the Bone Man's finger. He dropped his bow and arrows and caught the heart in the basket. He began to run. Behind him he heard the Bone Man rising, bone upon bone, as he had in Nulwee's dream, to chase the boy. The ground was rumbling. Nulwee's heart was thudding.

Nulwee ran as quickly as he could. The Bone Man followed, but without his heart, his body had no power. Kokolimalayas stumbled. His bones came apart, tumbling, and filled the riverbed.

Nulwee lifted the heart and called out, "Kokolimalayas, you made a lot of noise when you were alive. Now you can make noise in the sky." He threw the heart into the sky. It whirled into the distance like a ball of fire. It thundered loudly and the rain began to fall. Nulwee began to sing:

Now I am a warrior.
The monster's heart is thunder.
Now the sky gives us rain.
And the earth will be abundant.

Later that day, Nulwee leaned against his grandmother's back and told her the story. She spoke. "Your mother dreamed that you would one day destroy the Bone Man. So she wrapped you in a blanket and sent us into the mountains. *Now* the story is ended."

The rains continued to fall and the river grew full again and people returned to the land. When Nulwee grew older he became a great chief. Whenever it thundered, he told the story of Kokolimalayas the Bone Man. He taught his children the songs of his grandmother, and they taught their children:

> *The land is green and beautiful.*
> *The riverbed is full.*
> *The people live safely.*

It has been that way ever since.

AUTHOR'S NOTE

The tale of the Bone Man was recorded by Jeremiah Curtin around 1900, when Modoc Indians were still living near Upper Klamath Lake in Oregon. The Modoc were known for their bravery, and the beauty and excellence of their basketry.

Through conversations with Vi Hilbert, a Salishan elder living in Seattle, Washington; my friend Simon Ortiz, a poet from Acoma Pueblo; and Ron Evans, a Chippewa Cree Keeper of the Talking Stick, the many-leveled meanings of Modoc stories were revealed to me. *The Bone Man* charts the education of a warrior of the heart (a warrior whose strength comes from compassion). Nulwee learns tradition and courage from his grandmother, confronts inner and outer fears, and saves his people by transforming evil into good.

In reconstructing the story for young audiences, I have tried to honor its native source while bringing alive the wisdom that speaks to all people. I am honored to bring this story to life again.

ARTIST'S NOTE

Little is known about the ancient Modoc Indians, except that they dressed in clothes woven of tule grass and lived in shelters called wickiups. Because their tools and clothing were often composed of natural elements, most of their artifacts have disintegrated over time. The Modoc tribe of Oklahoma suggested I study Odie B. and Laura E. Faulk's book, *Modoc* (Chelsea House, 1988), from which I retrieved pictures of Modoc caps and baskets. I worked with one of the only existing photographs of a wickiup and a grinding stone. My friend Jim Filz, who was at one point the Secretary of the Massachusetts State Archery Association, supplied me with advice on how Native Americans held their arrows using the thumb grip—in contrast to today's common three-finger grip. Drawing the near-skeletal Kokolimalayas was a challenge. I hadn't drawn so many skeletons and half-dressed people in my life! What helped was a physical therapist's miniature skeleton, which I used as a model. I hope that my efforts will assist in bringing this fascinating story back to life, just as the landscape in Nulwee's time sprang back to life after the dark rule of the wicked Kokolimalayas.